Michael and His New Baby Brother

By Sarah, Duchess of York

Illustrated by Ian Cunliffe

STERLING

New York / London

STERLING and the distinctive Sterling logo are registered trademarks of
Sterling Publishing Co., Inc.

Library of Congress Cataloging-in-Publication Data

York, Sarah Mountbatten-Windsor, Duchess of, 1959-
[Thomas and his new baby brother]
Michael and his new baby brother / by Sarah, Duchess of York ; illustrated by Ian Cunliffe.
p. cm. -- (Helping hand)
Summary: Michael meets his baby brother and finds that he enjoys the new addition to the
family. Includes note to parents.
ISBN 978-1-4027-7390-7
[1. Babies--Fiction. 2. Brothers--Fiction.] I. Cunliffe, Ian, ill. II. Title.
PZ7.Y823Mi 2010
[E]--dc22
2009042145

Lot#:
2 4 6 8 10 9 7 5 3 1
04/10
Published by Sterling Publishing Co., Inc.
387 Park Avenue South, New York, NY 10016
Story and illustrations © 2007 by Startworks Ltd
'Ten Helpful Hints' © 2009 by Startworks Ltd
Distributed in Canada by Sterling Publishing
c/o Canadian Manda Group, 165 Dufferin Street
Toronto, Ontario, Canada M6K 3H6
Distributed in Australia by Capricorn Link (Australia) Pty. Ltd.
P.O. Box 704, Windsor, NSW 2756, Australia

Sterling ISBN 978-1-4027-7390-7

For information about custom editions, special sales, premium and
corporate purchases, please contact Sterling Special Sales
Department at 800-805-5489 or specialsales@sterlingpublishing.com.

All children face many new experiences as they grow up, and helping them to understand and deal with each is one of the most demanding and rewarding things we do as parents. Helping Hand Books are for both children and parents to read, perhaps together. Each simple story describes a childhood experience and shows some of the ways in which to make it a positive one. I do hope these books encourage children and parents to talk about these sometimes difficult issues. Talking together goes a long way to finding a solution.

Sarah,

Sarah, Duchess of York

Michael's mommy had big news.

One day after school, she sat Michael down and asked him to touch her tummy.

"Can you feel a bump?" she asked. "That's your baby brother or sister."

Michael touched his mommy's tummy again—but this time much more carefully.

Michael soon forgot about the "bump."

He didn't really want to think about it too much because
he was very happy with Mommy and Daddy and there was no
need for anyone else in the family.

He liked things just the way they were.

So when Mommy asked him if he was excited about the new baby, he wasn't sure.

"Let me tell you something, Michael," said his mommy. "I know that our new baby loves you very much already and that you are going to love him or her just as much too."

One day, when the "bump" had grown very big, Mommy had to go to the hospital so that the baby could be born. Grandpa came over to look after Michael. Early the next day, Daddy rushed into Michael's room and said, "Come on, Michael, get dressed as quickly as you can. We're going to the hospital to see Mommy and…your new baby brother, Daniel!"

Michael was very happy to have a brother. He wasn't so sure about sisters!

When they arrived at the hospital, Michael was so pleased to see his mommy that he hardly noticed the little bundle in the crib at the side of her bed. His mommy was thrilled to see him and gave him the biggest hug.

"Did you have a good day yesterday?" she asked. "What did you and Grandpa do?"

Just then, there was a gurgle from the crib and Michael looked at his baby brother for the first time. Daniel was moving his tiny arm.

Propped up at the end of the crib was a package wrapped in shiny paper.

"Daniel is saying hello to you," said Michael's mommy gently. "And I think he has a present for you."

Michael was surprised that a baby so small could have a present for him already, but decided not to ask too many questions!

His mommy passed the package to Michael, who opened it excitedly.

It was a space ship! All his friends had one.

"Oh, thank you, Daniel!" said Michael.

Michael thought about the fun he and Daniel would have playing together when his brother grew up.

"Michael," said his daddy, "I thought you might like to give Daniel the present you chose to welcome him into the world."

Michael gave Daniel a cuddly blue bear.

A little later, Daddy and Michael said goodbye to Mommy and Daniel, who had to stay in the hospital to rest.

"Time for you and me to go home," said Daddy. "We need to get things ready for this little bundle."

WELCOME HOME, DANIEL

Two days later, Mommy and Daniel came home from the hospital.

Michael had made a big sign for over the front door that said, "WELCOME HOME, DANIEL."

As soon as they were in the house, Mommy said, "Now, Michael, I'm going to need your help a lot to look after Daniel."

Michael wasn't sure what that meant, but he was very glad to be asked.

Later that day, Mommy said, "It's time to give Daniel a bath."
"He can play with all my bath toys!" suggested Michael.
"Daniel is a bit small for the big bath," said Mommy. "We'll use the one you had when you were a tiny baby."

Daniel wiggled when Michael helped to undress him and squealed when he first went into the water. Michael stroked him softly with the washcloth and he was soon smiling again.

"You're good at this," said Mommy. "You can help every bath time!"

Over the next few days, a lot of people came to the house to see the new baby.

"Michael," said his daddy, "will you please take everyone to see Daniel? You are already his best friend and he will be glad to have you there when he meets all these people for the first time."

So Michael took them all—uncles and aunts, friends and neighbors, Grandma and Grandpa—to see Daniel.

Each time, he would say something to his brother like, "Daniel, this is Peter and Anne. They're our neighbors. They're very nice and don't even mind when my baseball goes into their yard."

All the visitors brought a gift for Daniel, and some even brought a gift for Michael, because he was a big brother for the first time.

That night, just before going to sleep, Michael thought about Daniel.

"I'm glad Daniel is here," Michael said as he closed his eyes. "I think he's going to fit in with Mommy and Daddy and me just fine."

TEN HELPFUL HINTS

FOR PARENTS WHEN A NEW BABY ARRIVES

By Dr. Richard Woolfson, PhD

1. Talk positively from the moment you first mention to your child that a new baby is on the way. Tell him the new baby loves him already and thinks he is a terrific older sibling.

2. Expect your older child to be anxious when visiting you for the first time in the maternity hospital after the birth. Do your best to ensure that your older child meets the baby with a warm, very special introduction by you.

3. Buy a gift for your older child and take it into the hospital with you. Place it beside the crib when your older child visits for the first time and try to arrange that your older child has a gift to give to the baby.

4. Talk to your child about all the things she has been doing in the last couple of days, so that it doesn't feel like the baby's arrival hogs all the attention. Don't be surprised or upset if your older child is not as interested in the new baby as she is in seeing you again after a day or two apart.

5. Involve your older child in looking after the baby, for instance, by fetching a diaper. The more your older child is involved in the care of the baby, the more he'll feel connected with his new sibling.

6.   Ask your visitors to help you. You will need all the help you can get, and giving people specific tasks makes it easier for them to know how to assist you.

7.   Give your older child the job of leading visitors into the baby's room, and let her explain all about the new baby. This way she gets lots of attention too, and feels like she's the "big one" at home.

8.   Avoid clashes. Of course you have to give your new baby lots of attention, but try to introduce your older child to this idea gradually. Ask family and friends to play with the older child while you are busy with the baby so that he does not feel left out. If there is no one else around to spend time with your older child, make sure you find whatever time you can to play with him, so that he knows he is still an important part of the family.

9.   Never compare your children. In temper, you may inadvertently compare one of your children with the other. Such comparisons are always divisive and can create tension between your children.

10. Treat each of your children as unique individuals with their own particular qualities. For instance, they probably have different preferences for toys and books. Encourage such differences.

Dr. Richard Woolfson is a child psychologist, working with children and their families. He is also an author and has written several books on child development and family life, in addition to numerous articles for magazines and newspapers. Dr. Woolfson runs training workshops for parents and child care professionals and appears regularly on radio and television. He is a Fellow of the British Psychological Society.

Helping Hand Books

Look for these other helpful books
to share with your child:

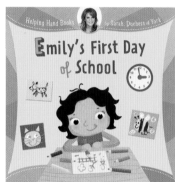